Disney's

DOUG™

Created by Jim Jinkins

CHRONICLES

A Picture for Patti

Linda K. Garvey

Illustrated by: Matthew C. Peters, Jeff Nodelman, Brian Donnelly

DISNEP PRESS

New York

Original characters for "The Funnies" developed by Jim Jinkins and Joe Aaron.

Printed in the United States of America.

3 5 7 9 10 8 6 4 2

The artwork for this book is prepared using watercolor.

The text for this book is set in 18-point New Century Schoolbook.

Library of Congress Catalog Card Number: 97-80214

ISBN:0-7868-4236-9

For more Disney Press fun, visit www.DisneyBooks.com

Disney's **DOUG**™

Created by
Jim Jinkins

CHRONICLES

A Picture for Patti

CHAPTER ONE

It was Friday afternoon, and the
final bell had rung at Beebe Bluff
Middle School. Doug Funnie walked
out of the building, depressed.

Patti hated him. She had
actually told him to leave her
alone. But Doug couldn't. He
followed her to Lucky Duck Park.
Patti was lying down in a small

clearing, staring at the sky.

Doug snuck from tree to tree, trying to get closer without her noticing him. But he tripped over a root, turned a somersault, and landed flat on his back about three feet from the girl of his dreams.

Oh, yeah. She noticed him all right.

"Oh, hi there, Patti. I was just . . ."

"Following me?" said Patti. "I thought I saw you behind me."

"Well, I had to, uh—"

"It's all right, Doug," she said wearily.

"Patti, are you okay?" Doug sat down next to her. He noticed that her nose was bright red. "Are you catching a cold or something?"

"No, Doug, I'm okay." She sniffed a little.

"Well, you look . . ." Doug knew something was wrong. He had made Patti Mayonnaise cry! "Uh, you're not crying, are you?"

Patti sat up, facing him. "No, I'm not crying. I guess I was pretty mean in school. I'm sorry. I feel kind of sad when the leaves change colors, that's all," she told him.

"Yeah, me, too. Summer's completely gone and the Swirly cycle goes into hibernation for the winter. It makes me sad, too," he agreed.

"No, it's not that. It's just . . . it's too hard to talk about, Doug. You wouldn't understand," she said.

Doug was insulted. He was "Mr.-Walk-a-Mile-in-My-Shoes"! Hadn't he understood when Coach Spitz wouldn't put her on the beetball team? He had even helped her form Patti's Pulverizers!

"I won't tell a soul, and I bet I *will* understand. Try me." Doug smiled his best Smash Adams smile.

"Well . . . did you ever lose something really important? That you loved a whole lot?"

"Yes!" Hah! He *did* understand! "I lost my wallet once."

She wasn't convinced. "I mean REALLY important. Something irreplaceable that you could never get back."

"Well, I almost lost Porkchop once. That was awful."

"That's a little closer to what I mean, but not quite it," Patti said. "I know you and Porkchop are best buddies. But, well . . . three years ago tomorrow, my mother died." Doug saw her nose turn an even brighter red. As she spoke, she fingered a locket around her neck. She wasn't looking at him.

"Oh." He knew he should say something. He had told her he would understand. But he didn't. He didn't have a clue what it would feel like to go home and have his mother not be there—ever!

"Oh," he said again. "Well, um, you seem . . . happ—uh, okay. You always look like you've gotten over . . ." Doug's voice trailed off as Patti glared at him. She stood.

"Doug Funnie!" she stormed.

"Losing your mother is not something you just GET OVER one day, and then life goes on as if it never happened! Life DOES go on, and a few days later, other people DO act like nothing ever happened. But *I'll* never feel the same again. It's not like losing your stuff! Losing a person is—well, it's just not like that!

"I knew you wouldn't understand! Just leave me alone!" She turned and ran away.

CHAPTER TWO

Doug was stunned. That was the second time Patti had told him to leave her alone! He had *really* blown it. She had shared personal things with him—BIG things, and he wanted her to share some more.

He walked home slowly, thinking. He had never thought about

how Patti must feel when she went home and her mom wasn't there. That meant there was no one to do stuff like bake the beet-berry pie for the holidays! Man!

But he did not want Patti to be mad at him. He wondered if she had ever talked to anyone else about this. He felt extra-special to think that she had confided only in him, Doug Funnie. And then he had blown it. Ahhhhhhgh!

Lost in his thoughts, Doug didn't notice the bus until Mr. Dink stepped off it.

"Hello, there, Douglas! Are you on your way home, my boy?" Mr. Dink always called him "my boy."

"Oh, hi, Mr. Dink. Yes, I am."
Doug thought for a moment. "Mr.
Dink, can I ask you a question?"

"Well, certainly, my boy. How
can I help you?"

"When someone . . . um, passes
on, how do you keep from forget-
ting what they were like?" Doug
asked him.

"Passes on what? The potatoes?"

"No," Doug explained. "Just passes on. Goes to heaven."

"Oh! You mean kicks the bucket? Buys the farm? Cashes in his chips? Checks out? You mean when someone . . . dies! It's okay to say the word, you know.

". . . Now, what was your question?"

Doug repeated it. "How do you remember what someone was like?"

"Now, let's see." Mr. Dink thought for a moment. "When my father, er, bought the farm, I kept his keys on my key ring. That way, every time I unlocked anything, I remembered him."

"Did it work?" Doug asked him.

"Well, it did until I lost my keys. In fact, that's why I'm taking the bus. Haven't been able to find those keys for months. I kind of like riding the bus, though. Reminds me of my father."

Doug couldn't remember why he was talking to Mr. Dink in the first place.

CHAPTER THREE

Still trying to understand how
Patti felt, Doug sat on his front
stoop to think. His mind drifted
off into a daydream.

Doug opened the front door. "I'm
home!" he called.

"I'm in the kitchen!" his father
answered. "Come see what I've got!"

"Hey, Dad," Doug said, joining

him. "What's that?" His dad was tinkering on some-thing he must have borrowed from Mr. Dink. It looked like a robot.

"This is Mabel, our new Super Dooper Megatronic Industrial Clean Machine," Phil told his son. "She dusts, vacuums, mops, scrubs bathrooms, does dishes, AND wakes everybody up in the morning. Judy's going to love her!"

At that very moment, his sister Judy staggered in from the garage loaded down with grocery bags. "Oh, no! What have you done to my kitchen!" she groaned. "Dad, get rid of that electric can opener so I can start supper. Doug, bring in the rest of the groceries!" She huffed and puffed, out of breath from her efforts.

Wow! Doug had never heard Judy speak like that to Dad—and get away with it! Doug wondered why Judy was shopping. Where was Mom, anyway? And Dirtbike? Maybe they were at the Déjà Vu Recycling Center.

By the time he came back with the groceries, Judy had recovered. "Hurry up, Dad! Get that pile of nuts and bolts out of here. Doug, help me get supper ready. Do I have to do everything? Come on, I'm not letting you guys make me miss another rehearsal! I've got better things to do than mother you two!"

By now, Doug was fed up. Judy always knew how to make him mad. "Well, who asked you to?" he challenged her. "Besides, who died and made *you* Queen Mother and Ruler of the Household?"

Judy stopped. She looked at her brother as if he were a complete numskull. "Oh, Doug! How could you be so cruel! *Mom* died!"

Ahhhhhhhgh! Doug snapped out of this horrible fantasy and went into his living room. There was good old Porkchop. He was the best nonhuman friend a boy ever had.

"Mom?" he called ner-vously.

"Douglas," Mom answered from the kitchen. "I've got some chocolate-covered peanutty banana cookies and milk here."

That was his mom, all right. She knew how to welcome a guy home after a hard day at school.

Doug ran in, grabbed two  cookies, and gave his mom a big giant hug. "I love you, Mom!" he said, biting into a cookie. He gave one to Porkchop.

"Mom?" he asked. "I have this friend whose mother . . . uh . . . kicked the bucket. No! She croaked. No! I mean . . ."

"Douglas, it's okay to say she died. It's something we need to learn to talk about out loud," his mother explained.

"But I don't know what to say! And now she thinks I don't understand! Mainly because I don't," he told her sadly.

"Well, son, she probably just wants you to listen. She has a lot of feelings to sort out, and sometimes it helps to say things out loud. You just need to be a good listener and show her you care," Mom suggested.

"Great idea, Mom!" Doug grabbed a handful of cookies and headed out the door. "Okay if I'm back by suppertime?"

Mom nodded. "Okay. And," she added, "be sure and tell Patti I said hello."

Doug blushed and ran out.

CHAPTER FOUR

Doug rang Patti's doorbell.

She opened the door.

He talked fast. "Hey, Patti, I'm sorry I wasn't a better listener. I know I blew it."

"That's okay. It's not easy for me to talk about it, anyway," she answered.

Doug gave her a chocolate-covered peanutty banana cookie. "Can we go to Bullseye Park and talk for a minute? I've been thinking about how I'd feel if *I* were you," he said. "You must miss your mom a lot."

Patti stopped chewing and looked at him. She blinked three times. "Yes, I do," she said. "It's hard to find anything that makes me feel better."

They walked down the street to the park and sat

on a bench.
Doug
thought
hard
this
time
before
he

said anything. He didn't want to say the wrong thing again!

"So, uh, is there anything that makes you feel better, even a little?"

"Well, my dad tells wonderful stories about Mama. Sometimes I sit in his lap and we look at pictures while he talks about stuff that happened before I was even born. Like when they first met at a sports camp in the Poulet Mountains. I love those stories. They cheer him up, too."

Doug gave her another cookie.

"And I love to think about what my mom told me when my grandaddy died." Patti began to look more cheerful.

"What did she tell you?" he asked.

"I was only six but I missed him a lot. Mama said it was okay, because only his body was gone. She said the part that made him be Grandaddy went to live with the angels. From heaven, he can watch me play beetball, watch me read a book, or whatever I do. He

even
cheers for
me to win
the
games I
play.
Mama
said I

may not hear him with my ears,
but if I listen real hard, I can
hear him with my heart."

Doug was quiet for a minute.
"Wow," he said.

"She told me I have work to do
here, but someday, after I've done
everything I'm supposed to do, I
can join him."

Patti went on. "I used to talk to

Mama and Daddy about how much Grandaddy misses us. He must have been glad to see Mama. I like to think about the two of them together, watching me."

"Cool," he said, impressed.

"The thing I miss most of all is the way Mama and I used to talk. Almost every night, at bedtime, I would tell her all about my day.

"For a long time after she was gone, I still talked to her at bed-

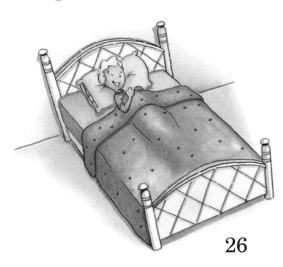

time. Sometimes when I closed my eyes, I could

imagine her voice saying the things I knew she'd say. It made me feel less lonely. It was better than looking at her pictures." She took another cookie.

"Oh, yeah," he said. "I saw one of those once when it fell out of your locker." In the picture, Patti and her mom were on their front porch. "She looked like you, only older."

Patti smiled at him and put her foot up on the bench. "But now I'm so busy that I fall asleep. I forget to talk to Mama for months at a time."

She looked sad again. "Maybe I just don't want to think about it. Once, I pretended that she was never here and I always lived with just Daddy. I felt awful after that.

"At first it was scary that she's not here anymore. But now I'm scared that if I don't think about her every single day, it'll seem like she was never real at all. One day I'll try to remember her, and

it will all seem like a fairy tale.

"I don't want to forget what she was like!"

Doug looked at his friend. This was a BIG problem. He was okay with little problems like, should I wear my green cotton sweater or my green wool sweater? Or how do we lure the Lucky Duck Monster out of hiding? But this problem was harder than anything he had ever faced!

What could he do to help Patti remember what her mother was like?

"Patti?" Doug couldn't think of anything to say again. "I better go home now. See ya."

CHAPTER FIVE

At home, Doug climbed the stairs to his room. "Well, Porkchop," he said, "I've got to come up with a great idea to help Patti remember what her mom was like."

Doug closed the door to his room. Porkchop hopped on the bed and curled up for a nap. Drowsily, he watched as his best

human friend lay down and took
out a Quailman comic.

A few minutes later, Doug's
thoughts were not on the comic
book in his hand. He was in
another fantasy.

Quailman was tied up, captured
by his archenemy, Dr. Rubbersuit.
The villainous Rubbersuit
laughed wickedly as he said, "I've

got you now, Belt-Brain! I am invincible! Soon, the whole world will be mine! Already, I command the memories of everyone at Beebe Bluff Middle School. Now they will remember only me, ME, ME!!!"

The Man of Rubber gloated. "I can even make you think that I'm your mother!"

"I didn't have a mother," Quailman told him sadly. "She flew away when I was just a baby chick."

Dr. Rubbersuit stopped short. "No mother? My father left when I was very small. No wonder we both wear such weird clothes.

Rubber makes you sweat and it itches, too. And look at you! You wear under-wear on the outside of your pants!"

"Power Briefs!" screamed Quailman. "They're Power Briefs!"

"Doug! Time for supper!" Doug's father's voice woke him from his daydream.

"Coming, Dad!" he answered. After the supper dishes were

done, he went back to his room to think. He still needed the perfect idea for the perfect girl. He had hoped to come up with one before bedtime, but he was tired. It had been a long day. He'd think about it when he woke up.

CHAPTER SIX

While he was sleeping, Doug dreamed that he and Patti were playing a game of Shot in the Dark.

Patti drew a card. "Okay, this is an easy one, Doug. You'll get this on the first clue. This person taught you more than anyone else."

"Mrs. Wingo?"

"No. This person takes you places every day."

"Dad?"

"Wrong. This is the one who helps you solve your most complicated problems."

"Uh, Mr. Dink?"

"Nope. Okay, it's a girl."

"I got it! Judy."

"Huh-uh. No, Doug, think!" Patti was getting impatient. "She never lets you down. She's always there when you need her! She *loves* you!"

Doug looked in amazement at the girl of his dreams. He couldn't believe this was happening! "You?"

Patti snorted. "Get real! Come on, Doug, I don't have all day."

Now, Doug was totally embarrassed and confused. In

desperation he began to guess wildly. "Miss Kristal? Beebe—NO! Not Beebe! Mrs. Dink? Connie?"

"No, no, no! Doug, it's your mom! How could you forget your own mother!! What a LOSER!"

Doug sat straight up in bed, instantly awake. Whoa! What an awful nightmare!

In a flash, he knew more about what Patti had been going through than ever before. Surely there was something he could do to help her. But what?

On top of the covers, Porkchop snored softly. Doug got carefully out of bed. He didn't want to disturb his friend. Outside, the

sun was rising.

He went to his desk and took out a No. 2 drawing pencil and some paper. This was a very hard problem, way harder than any he had ever tackled!

He started to doodle. His best ideas came when he had a pencil in his hand.

He looked down at the paper.

Suddenly, he knew exactly what to do.

CHAPTER SEVEN

Doug was almost ready to leave the house. But first, he had a few things to do.

Mom was playing with Dirtbike in the backyard.

"Mom?" he began. "I'm going over to Patti's for a little while, okay?"

"Okay, Douglas. Be back by five."

He stood nervously for a few seconds. Suddenly, he hugged his mom and Dirtbike. "I love you, Mom! I love you, Dirtbike!" Then he ran to the garage door.

His mother shook her head and smiled.

In the garage, Phil Funnie leaned under the hood of the car.

"Dad?" he said. "I need to tell you something."

Doug's dad stood up, holding a screwdriver in one greasy hand. "What is it, son?" he asked.

Doug was nervous again. "Dad, I love you!" he blurted. Then he ran back into the house, leaving Phil with a confused look on his face.

Judy was in the living room, studying lines for her one-person show called *Ju-dy, or Not Ju-dy*. Doug stood by the door, wondering if this was a good idea. After a few minutes he squared his shoulders and entered.

"Judy? I lo . . . I lov . . . uh, you're okay!" he said, and ran

outside. Whew! He was glad that
was over!

In the living room, Judy
grinned and yelled after him,
"Yeah? Well, I love you, too, little
brother."

CHAPTER EIGHT

Doug and Porkchop rang Patti's
doorbell.

Suddenly, Doug wished he had
stayed home. This had seemed
like such a good idea back in his
room, but now he wasn't so sure.
What if she hated it?

Patti's father invited them into
the living room and Patti joined

them. Oh, if only he could think of something clever to say! What would Smash Adams say?

"Here, Patti," he said, handing her a flat paper bag with something in it.

Oh, great, Doug, he thought to himself. *That* was clever.

Porkchop moaned softly. Doug knew if his dog could talk, he would know exactly what to say.

A long, breathless moment passed while Patti pulled out the piece of art paper and stared at it. Mr. Mayonnaise looked at it, too. "Oh, Doug," he said.

Doug's heart sank. He thought it was a good idea but he was wrong. They couldn't even speak.

For the kazillionth time, he plunged into a nightmarish fantasy. Doug stood with Patti in the conductor's cab of a runaway train. The train raced toward a fork in the tracks.

He pulled the brakes. Nothing happened.

"Looks like the brakes are out!" he told Patti. "We've got to decide which track to take!"

"Oh, Doug," Patti responded anxiously. "I remember this fork. One way leads to the old collapsed Noodle River Bridge and certain death; the other is the new New Hamster line and we'll be home for supper. But I don't know which is which! You decide, Doug! You're so . . . so . . . good judgment-y!"

Doug spoke up, sure of himself. "Why thank you, Patti. I will. Let's go left. Left has always been good for me. I'm left-handed, you know." Confidently, he made the adjustment.

The train veered left. The two

friends watched breathlessly.
Sparks flew as the train raced
past the fork.

Rounding a bend, the collapsed
trestles of the Noodle River Bridge

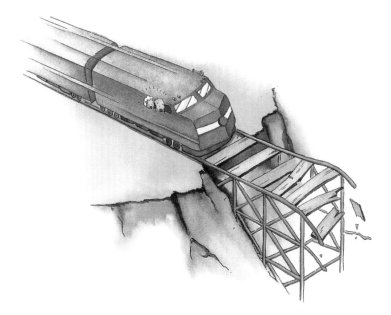

came suddenly into view. "Oh,
great," said Patti. "Not only are we
gonna miss supper, we're doomed!"

Doug had blown it. He should have chosen right, not left! He did the only thing he could do. Panic. "Ahhhhhhh!"

Back in her living room, Patti burst into tears. Doug came crashing down into a reality that was even worse than his fantasy. He had made the most perfect girl in the universe cry!

Doug's shoulders slumped. Oh, if only he could disappear in a puff of smoke!

"Oh, Doug," Patti said, through her tears. Her eyes were still on the picture Doug had drawn. "It's so beautiful, I . . . I don't know what to say." Her voice quivered.

Mr. Mayonnaise spoke up. His voice sounded kind of funny, too. "Doug, what a thoughtful gift. It cheers me up. Patti's mom would have loved it."

Now Doug really didn't know what to say! But at least he was not a big loser!

"Well, uh, we . . . have to, um . . ."
Porkchop groaned and slapped
his paw to his forehead. Doug
knew he was stammering, but he
couldn't stop himself. In his day-
dreams, he was
smooth and cool
like Smash Adams.
But in real life, he
always ended up
just being himself.
Doug.

"Doug? Thank
you. You'll never
know how much this picture
means to me." Patti hadn't
stopped looking at it yet. She
really did like it!

CHAPTER NINE

Patti stood by her dad as
Porkchop closed the door. She sat
on his lap and they both looked at
the picture. "Wow," she said. "This
is wonderful. What a great guy."

"Yeah, he's a good friend to you,
isn't he?" replied her dad. He
hugged his little girl tightly. "He
must understand how much we

miss Mama, especially today."

"Yes, I think he does," she said, hugging him back. "This picture reminds me that, one day, even if it's a very long time away, we'll get to be with her and Grandaddy. That makes me feel good."

"Yeah, me, too," said Chad Mayonnaise. "Do you want to

frame it and hang it in your room?"

"That's a great idea!" said Patti. "I think I'll take it up to see how it'll look there."

Giving him a big squeeze, she climbed down and raced to her room. With a thumbtack, she carefully pinned the picture to

the spot where she could see it every day. She sat down on the bed to see how it looked.

"Well, Mama," she said, "I miss you a whole lot—and Grandaddy, too. I get so lonely sometimes that I just have to think about something else for a while. But that doesn't mean I don't love you.

"Mama, I've got this great friend, Doug. You'd like him a lot. And he's got a really smart dog . . ."

EPILOGUE

Dear Journal,

Hey, it's me, Doug. Today I found out that sometimes when people act mad at you, they're really upset about something that happened to them.

Maybe you never completely get over losing someone you love. Patti says it hurts a little bit less every day, until you can stand it, most of the time.

Anyway, I hope Patti's having a LONNNGGG talk with her mom right now!

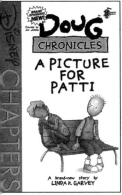
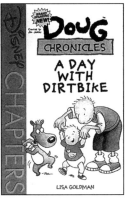

Doug, Patti, Skeeter, Soft Friends From Mattel!